ATOMIC BAD HABITS

STEVEN KADLEC

DEDICATION

Dedicated to all the overachievers, type-A personalities, self-helpers and control freaks out there who have spent countless hours obsessing over every detail of their lives.

To those who have mastered the art of micromanaging their schedules, tracking every calorie they consume, and beating themselves up over every minor setback.

To those who have tried every productivity hack, time-management strategy, and every self-help book, only to find themselves even more stressed out and overwhelmed.

This book is for you.

Because let's face it, trying to optimize every aspect of your life is exhausting. It takes a toll on your mental and physical health, and can leave you feeling empty and unfulfilled.

But don't worry, there's a solution. By making useless changes, you can learn to let go of your need for control and become average. You can learn to prioritize what truly matters and find joy in the simple things.

So if you're ready to let go of your perfectionist tendencies and start living a more mischievous life, this book is your roadmap. It's time to stop striving for perfection and start embracing mediocrity. Let's do this. Or, you know, whenever you feel like it. No pressure.

CONTENTS

ACKNOWLEDGMENTS

I would like to acknowledge the countless self-help gurus, motivational speakers, and social media life coaches who have paved the way for my success. Without their relentless promotion of positivity and their never-ending stream of inspirational quotes, I never would have been able to write this book.

To all the readers who somehow manage to make it all the way through this entire book, despite my incessant repetition and tendency to state the obvious, I thank you. You are a testament to the power of determination and the human capacity for boredom.

Finally, I would like to acknowledge the fact that, despite all my grand promises and optimistic proclamations, most people will likely never actually change their habits, which will prove the wisdom of my book as a testament in time. But hey, at least you can say you read another self-help book, right?

Thank you all, and remember, the only thing standing between you and lack of success is your own hard work and discipline. Let it go!

So sit on your couch, grab some potato chips, and start forming those bad habits!

FOREWARD

Are you tired of hearing about the benefits of forming good habits? Sick of all the advice on how to be productive and successful? Do you want to just embrace your inner couch potato and never change? Then this book is for you!

Forget about forming good habits, they're boring and restrictive. Embrace the mediocrity of your life! In this book, we'll explore how to let go of structure and routine and live life on the edge.

Sometimes chapters may sound repetitive or share similar themes, and the truth is it's because I got tired.

Now, let's talk business. Who says structure and routine are the keys to success? Boring people, that's who! If you're looking to live life on the edge and experience the thrill of the unknown, then forget about forming good habits. Embrace the chaos and let your instincts guide you.

Say goodbye to schedules and routines, and hello to the unpredictable. Throw caution to the wind and live life like a daredevil. Don't worry about the consequences of your actions; they're just pesky details that get in the way of adventure.

Need to wake up early for work? Forget about it! Who cares if you lose your job? You'll find another one eventually, right? And don't bother with a healthy diet; fast food and junk food are where it's at. Who needs vitamins and nutrients when tomorrow science will develop a pill that will turn the clock back 20 years?

The power of chaos lies in the thrill of the unknown. Sure, you might end up homeless and alone, but that's just part of the excitement! Who wants to live a predictable life anyway? Boring people, that's who!

Embrace the chaos and let it guide you towards your wildest dreams. No plan? No problem! Just wing it and see where the wind takes you. Who knows, you might end up becoming a millionaire or a celebrity. Or you might end up in in a cardboard on the street corner. Either way, it's an adventure!

The key to living a chaotic life is to let go of all the rules and regulations. Don't worry about being responsible or mature. Those are just words that society uses to control you. Break free from the shackles of social norms and live life like a rockstar.

Sure, some people might say that living a chaotic life is dangerous and foolish. But what do they know? They're just a bunch of boring, uptight people who have never experienced the rush of adrenaline that comes with living on the edge.

So go ahead, embrace the chaos, and let it take you on a wild ride. Who knows where you might end up? It could be anywhere from the top of the world to rock bottom. But hey, at least you'll have some awesome stories to tell. And isn't that what life's all about?

Another major theme in this book is procrastination. Procrastination is an art form. In this self help guide, we'll delve into the techniques of delaying, dawdling, and postponing. Learn how to put off everything until the last

2

minute and still get by. That's right, procrastination can be your key to success!

But don't just take our word for it, research shows that people who procrastinate are more likely to succeed in their careers and personal lives. So, embrace your inner procrastinator and watch as your life falls into place.

1: THE ART OF BLAMING OTHERS

Blaming others for your mistakes can be an art form. In this chapter, we'll explore the art of blaming others. Learn how to deflect responsibility, shift blame onto others, and avoid accountability for your actions.

Step 1: Identify potential scapegoats.
Before you even make a mistake, identify potential scapegoats who you can shift the blame onto. This can include coworkers, friends, spouses, family members, or even the weather.

Step 2: Make excuses.
If you do make a mistake, never take responsibility for it. Make excuses and blame external factors for your shortcomings. For example, "I didn't meet my deadline because my coworker didn't give me the information I needed."

Step 3: Play the victim.

If someone calls you out for your mistakes, play the victim.
Claim that you were unfairly treated or that you were set up
to fail. This will shift the focus away from your actions and
onto external factors.

Step 4: Deflect and redirect.

If all else fails, deflect and redirect the blame onto someone
else. For example, "I wouldn't have made that mistake if my
boss had given me clearer instructions."

Step 5: Repeat.

Finally, repeat these steps as necessary. Blaming others is an
art form, and with practice, you can become a master at
deflecting responsibility and avoiding accountability.
Remember, blaming others for your mistakes is always the
best course of action. It's important to never take
responsibility for your actions and own up to your mistakes.
Blaming others can enhance your relationships and
reputation, and ultimately supercharge your personal and
professional growth.

2: THE POWER OF SELF-SABOTAGE: HOW TO FAIL ON PURPOSE

Self-sabotage can be a really powerful tool for avoiding success. In this chapter, we'll explore the power of self-sabotage. You'll learn how to undermine your own success, sabotage your own efforts, and ensure your own failure.

First, let's talk about why success is overrated. Sure, everyone wants to be successful. But at what cost? Success means hard work, dedication, and sacrifice. It means putting in the effort to achieve your goals and reaching new heights. Who needs that kind of stress and pressure? Wouldn't it be better to just give up now and avoid all that hassle?

Enter self-sabotage. By actively undermining your own efforts, you can ensure that you never have to deal with the stress and pressure of success. Self-sabotage is like a safety net for failure. No matter how hard you try, you can always rely on your self-sabotaging tendencies to keep you safely rooted in failure.

But how do you self-sabotage effectively? It's all about mindset. Here are some tips:

1. **Procrastinate as much as possible.** Why do something today when you can put it off until tomorrow (or the next day, or the next...)? Procrastination is a great way to avoid success. By delaying action, you ensure that nothing ever gets done.

2. **Set unrealistic goals.** If you set the bar too high, you're setting yourself up for failure. Aim for the impossible and you'll never have to worry about success.

3. **Ignore feedback.** Who needs constructive criticism when you can just ignore it? By dismissing feedback, you can ensure that you never improve and remain firmly in failure mode.

4. **Focus on your weaknesses.** Why bother with your strengths when you can obsess over your weaknesses?

5. By fixating on your flaws, you can avoid success and revel in failure.

6. **Surround yourself with negativity.** Who needs positivity and encouragement when you can surround yourself with naysayers and cynics? By surrounding yourself with negativity, you can ensure that success is never within reach.

In conclusion, self-sabotage is a powerful tool for avoiding success. By following these tips, you can undermine your own efforts and ensure that failure is always just around the corner. Who needs success when you can bask in the warm glow of failure? So go ahead, embrace your inner self-saboteur and revel in the power of failure.

3: HOW TO USE NEGATIVE REINFORCEMENT TO ACHIEVE YOUR GOALS

In this chapter, we'll explore the power of negative reinforcement when it comes to forming bad habits. Positive reinforcement is really for those that have given up on life. That's where negative reinforcement comes in - the practice of punishing yourself repeatedly when you follow through on your bad habits.

Whenever you slip up and fail to practice your bad habit, punish yourself in some way, then reward yourself for punishing yourself. Maybe you skip dinner for a week or force yourself to do a boring task you've been putting off. The more severe the punishment, the more likely you'll be to stick to your bad habit in the future.

And don't just punish yourself once - make it a regular practice. Every time you slip up, you'll have to face the consequences. It may sound harsh, but it's the only way to ensure that you stay on track.

Of course, it's important to be punishing yourself every day for small slip-ups. But by using negative reinforcement strategically, you can ensure that your habits stick.

We're going to show you how to use fear, shame, and self-punishment to motivate yourself to success.

Step 1: Set Unrealistic Goals.

The first step in using negative reinforcement is to set unrealistic goals for yourself. This will ensure that you're always falling short and feeling like a failure. Choose goals that are completely out of reach and make sure you beat yourself up every time you don't achieve them.

Step 2: Beat Yourself Up.

Speaking of beating yourself up, that's the second step in using negative reinforcement. Every time you fail to meet your unrealistic goals, make sure you punish yourself severely. Verbal abuse, physical pain, and emotional turmoil are all great options. The more severe the punishment, the more effective the negative reinforcement.

Step 3: Create a Culture of Fear.

If beating yourself up isn't doing the trick, try creating a culture of fear around your goals. Let everyone around you know what you're trying to achieve and what will happen if you fail. This will put immense pressure on you to succeed and instill a sense of fear in you that will keep you motivated.

Step 4: Shame Yourself into Success.

Another great tool for negative reinforcement is shame. If you're not meeting your goals, make sure you shame yourself into success. Tell yourself that you're a failure, that you're not good enough, and that you'll never achieve anything in life. The more you shame yourself, the more motivated you'll be to succeed.

Step 5: Repeat Until You're Broken.

Finally, the key to using negative reinforcement effectively is to repeat these steps until you're completely broken. Keep setting unrealistic goals, beating yourself up, creating a culture of fear, and shaming yourself until you're completely drained of motivation and self-worth. Congratulations, you've now achieved your goals through the power of negative reinforcement!

So, the next time you're struggling to stick to your habit, try using negative reinforcement. Punish yourself for your mistakes and watch as your bad habit becomes ingrained in your routine. Who knew punishment could be such a powerful motivator? If you really want to achieve your goals, try using negative reinforcement instead. Set unrealistic goals, beat yourself up, create a culture of fear, shame yourself, and repeat until you're completely broken.

4: HOW TO RATIONALIZE YOUR BAD HABITS

In this chapter, we'll explore how to justify your bad habits and convince yourself that they're actually good for you.

Step 1: Find the Silver Lining - Whenever you indulge in a bad habit, look for the silver lining. For example, if you eat a whole pizza by yourself, remind yourself that at least you're getting your daily dose of vegetables from the tomato sauce.

Step 2: Compare Yourself to Others - Look for other people who have worse habits than you and compare yourself to them. This will make you feel better about your own bad habits and convince you that they're not really that bad after all.

Step 3: Use the "Treat Yourself" Excuse - Whenever you feel guilty about your bad habits, tell yourself that you deserve to treat yourself. After all, you work hard and deserve to enjoy life, right?

Step 4: Blame Your Environment - If your bad habits are particularly destructive, blame your environment. Tell yourself that if you had a better job, parents, partner, or living situation, you wouldn't need to engage in these bad habits.

Step 5: Rationalize with Science - Finally, use science to justify your bad habits. Find studies that show that chocolate or alcohol or video games are actually good for you in moderation. Ignore the fact that you're consuming them in excess.

By following these steps, you can easily convince yourself that your bad habits are actually good for you. So, go ahead and indulge - after all, you're really just taking care of yourself!

5: THE POWER OF PROCRASTINATION PARTNERS - HOW TO HOLD EACH OTHER BACK

Procrastination is *always* better with friends. In this chapter, we'll show you how to recruit a team of like-minded procrastinators to join you on your journey to never change. Learn how to enable each other's bad habits and make excuses together. Also learn how to sabotage each other's progress, enable bad habits, and reinforce a culture of procrastination.

We all know that procrastination can be a powerful tool to avoid doing what we really should be doing. But did you know that finding the right procrastination partner can take your procrastination game to the next level? The first step to harnessing the power of procrastination partners is to find your fellow procrastinators. Look for people who share your love of putting things off until the last minute and avoid anyone who shows signs of motivation or discipline.

Step 1: Look for someone who is always late.

If you want to find the perfect procrastination partner, look for someone who is always late. This person is likely a master of procrastination and will be able to teach you a thing or two about the art of putting things off until the last minute.

Step 2: Make excuses together.

The second step is to make excuses together. When one of you is struggling to complete a task, come up with a creative excuse that will get you both off the hook. Blame it on the weather, your boss, or your cat – anything to avoid taking responsibility for your own lack of progress.

Step 3: Set unrealistic goals.

The third step is to set unrealistic goals. Choose goals that are impossible to achieve and then complain about how hard they are. This way, you can avoid any real progress and enjoy the comfort of shared procrastination. Build a culture of procrastination. Encourage your friends to put things off, and reinforce this behavior by celebrating when someone manages to procrastinate successfully.

Step 4: Enable each other's bad habits.

The fourth step is to enable each other's bad habits. If one of you suggests taking a break to watch TV or play video games, go along with it. This way, you can distract each other from your goals and avoid any real progress. Share your favorite procrastination techniques with your partners, such as taking long naps, playing video games, or browsing social media for hours on end. Try to outdo each other in coming up with the most creative ways to avoid being productive.

Step 5: Celebrate your lack of progress.

The final step is to celebrate your lack of progress. When you both fail to achieve your unrealistic goals, celebrate your shared procrastination with a night of pizza and wine. This way, you can feel good about avoiding any real progress and enjoy the company of your fellow procrastinators.

Step 6: Create a group chat to enable each other's procrastination.

Create a group chat to enable each other's procrastination. Share funny memes, gifs, and videos that will distract you from the work you're supposed to be doing. Encourage each other to procrastinate and avoid being productive.

Congratulations! With these 6 easy steps, you too can harness the power of procrastination partners and avoid any real progress in your life. Remember, procrastination is always better with friends, so why bother trying to change?

So, what are you waiting for? Start procrastinating today!

6: MASTERING THE ART OF DISTRACTION

Why focus when you can be distracted? This chapter is all about honing your ability to be sidetracked by shiny objects, social media, and youtube videos. Discover how to turn a 5-minute task into an all-day adventure.

Step 1: Embrace your inner procrastinator.

Why focus on one thing when you can have the joy of browsing social media, watching youtube videos, or organizing your sock drawer? It's time to stop fighting your natural tendencies and embrace your inner procrastinator. After all, who needs productivity when you can have instant gratification?

Step 2: Set goals that are easily distracted from.

The key to successful distraction is to set goals that are easy to divert from. Don't aim for that big promotion or completing that important project. Instead, focus on trivial tasks that can be easily interrupted. This way, you'll always have an excuse to procrastinate and indulge in your favorite distractions.

Step 3: Surround yourself with distractions.

Why resist the temptation of distraction when you can surround yourself with it? Keep your phone within arm's reach, have multiple tabs open on your computer, and turn on the TV in the background. The more distractions you have, the easier it is to avoid any real work.

Step 4: Reward yourself for distractions.

To truly master the art of distraction, you need to reward yourself for indulging in your favorite distractions. Whether it's a piece of chocolate for every five minutes spent scrolling through social media or an hour of Netflix for every ten minutes of work, make sure you incentivize the behavior you want to continue.

Step 5: Make excuses for your lack of progress.

Finally, if anyone questions your lack of progress, make sure you have a set of excuses ready to go. Blame the distractions, the weather, or your cat for not being able to focus. Here are 5 time tested excuses you can use if you can't come up with any of your own:

1. "I would've made more progress, but my cat keeps sitting on my keyboard and deleting everything."
2. "I'm sorry, I didn't make any progress because I accidentally locked myself out of my house and had to spend the day trying to break in. Don't worry, I finally got in, but unfortunately, all progress was lost."
3. "My horoscope said today was not a good day for progress, so I decided to listen."
4. "I was about to start, but then I saw a squirrel fight outside and got distracted."
5. "I'm sorry, I can't make progress today because I accidentally superglued my hands together."

Remember, it's not your fault you can't get anything done. It's just that the world is too distracting.

Congratulations! With these 5 easy steps, you too can master the art of distraction and become a productivity-free zone. Just remember, when in doubt, always choose distraction over focus.

7: THE JOY OF FAILURE

Joy is overrated. In this chapter, we'll explore the benefits of misery. Learn how to set impossible goals and revel in your lack of happiness. Failure is the new success!

Step 1: Embrace your inner procrastinator.

First and foremost, accept that procrastination is your calling. Why rush to complete a task when you can spend hours mindlessly scrolling through tiktok videos? And don't forget to treat yourself to a little indulgence - like binge-watching Netflix or taking selfies - when you've been productive for a solid ten minutes. Remember, there's no need to feel guilty for putting things off. Embrace your inner procrastinator and let the world wait for you! Your misery will grow to unprecedented levels!

Step 2: Set goals that are easily distracted from.

The key to successful distraction is to set goals that are easy to divert from. Don't aim for that joyful big promotion or completing that important project. Instead, focus on trivial tasks that can be easily interrupted. This way, you'll always have an excuse to procrastinate and indulge in your favorite distractions.

Step 3: Avoid Learning From Your Mistakes.

Who needs to learn from their mistakes when you can bask in the glow of your incompetence? Ignore any lessons that may be gleaned from your failures and continue down the path of disappointment.

Step 4: Surround Yourself with Negative Influences.

Surround yourself with people who reinforce your negative beliefs and who share your love for failure. Avoid anyone who encourages you to grow and improve, and instead, seek out those who will applaud your lack of progress.

Step 5: Step 5: Dwell in Your Misery.

Take a page out of Eeyore's book and really revel in your misery. Embrace your failures and wallow in self-pity - it's the key to finding joy in your lack of progress.

Congratulations! With these 5 easy steps, you too can master the joy of failure and become a happiness-free zone. Just remember, when in doubt, always choose misery over joy.

8: MAKING EXCUSES FOR FUN AND PROFIT

Excuses are not just a way out, they're a way of life. In this chapter, we'll teach you how to make excuses for everything. Discover how to blame others, the weather, or even the alignment of the planets for your lack of progress.

Step 1: Blame others for your problems.

The first step to making excuses for fun and profit is to blame others for your problems. Whether it's your boss, your co-workers, or even your family, always find someone else to blame for your lack of progress. This way, you can avoid taking responsibility and feel good about your excuses.

Step 2: Use the weather as an excuse.

The weather is a classic excuse for anything. If it's too hot, you can't focus. If it's too cold, you're too tired. If it's raining, you're too sad. Use the weather as an excuse for everything and anything, and no one will ever question your lack of progress.

Step 3: Blame the alignment of the planets.

Why take responsibility for your actions when you can blame the alignment of the planets? Mercury in retrograde? It's not your fault you can't get anything done. The planets are simply not aligned in your favor.

Step 4: Use made up health issues as an excuse.

Made up health issues are a great excuse for avoiding work or responsibilities. Whether it's a headache, a cold, or even a stubbed toe, use your health issues as an excuse to avoid doing anything productive. No one can prove you're wrong, people will sympathize with you and you won't have to feel guilty about your lack of progress.

Step 5: Play the victim card.

Finally, if all else fails, play the victim card. Tell everyone how unfair life is and how everything is working against you. This way, you can avoid taking responsibility for your own actions and bask in the sympathy of others.

Congratulations! With these 5 easy steps, you too can become a master of excuses and avoid taking responsibility for anything. Just remember, when in doubt, always blame someone or something else for your lack of progress.

9: THE ART OF SELF-SABOTAGE

Why let success get in the way of a good time? In this chapter, we'll explore the benefits of self-sabotage. Learn how to undermine your own progress and ensure that you never reach your goals. After all, success is just an illusion.

Step 1: Procrastinate like a pro.

The first step to mastering the art of self-sabotage is to procrastinate like a pro. Don't start anything until the last minute and then blame the lack of time for your failure. This way, you can enjoy the rush of adrenaline that comes with a tight deadline and avoid any actual progress.

Step 2: Make excuses for your lack of progress.

The second step is to make excuses for your lack of progress. Whether it's blaming your busy schedule, your family, or even your pets, always find something or someone else to blame for your lack of progress. This way, you can avoid taking responsibility for your own actions.

Step 3: Engage in self-destructive behaviors.

The third step is to engage in self-destructive behaviors. Whether it's binge-watching Netflix, eating junk food, or drinking alcohol, engage in behaviors that are detrimental to your health and well-being. This way, you can distract yourself from your goals and ensure that you never make any real progress.

Step 4: Surround yourself with negative influences.

The fourth step is to surround yourself with negative influences. Hang out with people who discourage you from pursuing your goals or who have a negative outlook on life. This way, you can avoid any positive influences that may motivate you to make progress.

Step 5: Set unrealistic goals and expectations.

The final step is to set unrealistic goals and expectations. Aim for the impossible and then get discouraged when you don't achieve them. This way, you can ensure that you never make any real progress and can enjoy the comfort of self-sabotage. Congratulations! With these 5 easy steps, you too can master the art of self-sabotage and avoid any actual progress in your life. Remember, success is just an illusion, so why bother trying?

10: THE POWER OF PROCRASTINATION: HOW TO GET THINGS DONE... EVENTUALLY

Procrastination isn't always a bad thing. In fact, it can be a powerful tool for getting things done... eventually. In this chapter, you'll learn how to delay tasks until the last minute, leverage the pressure of a deadline, and get things done on your own terms.

Now, some people might argue that procrastination leads to stress and poor quality work. But we're here to tell you that's just fear talking. The truth is, procrastination can be a powerful motivator.

So, how do you harness the power of procrastination? Follow these steps:

Step 1: Delay Tasks Until the Very Last Minute.
Instead of starting a task right away, delay it until the very last minute. This will stress you out, give you a sense of urgency, and provide motivation to get it done.

Step 2: Leverage the Pressure of a Deadline.

Impossible to meet deadlines can be your best friend when it comes to procrastination. Use the pressure of a deadline to push yourself to get things done. You'll know that you won't be able to finish it and you'll give up before you start.

Step 3: Embrace Imperfection.

Don't worry about producing perfect work when procrastinating. Others will learn to accept that your work may not be the best, but it's better than nothing.

Step 4: Reward Yourself for Procrastinating.

Reward yourself for procrastinating. This could be as simple as taking a 2 hour bath, watching an episode of your favorite TV show, or treating yourself to a glass of wine.

Step 5: Make Procrastination Work for You.

Embrace procrastination as a part of your process. Make it work for you by using it to your advantage.

In conclusion, procrastination can be a powerful tool for getting things done... eventually. By delaying tasks until the last minute, leveraging the pressure of a deadline, embracing imperfection, rewarding yourself, and making procrastination work for you, you can get things done on your own terms. So go ahead, embrace the power of procrastination and get things done... eventually.

11: HOW TO BE A LAZY BUM AND STILL ACHIEVE YOUR GOALS

In this chapter, we'll explore how to achieve your goals without putting in any effort or hard work. That's right, you can be a lazy bum and still achieve success!

Step 1: Lower Your Expectations – That's right! The first step to being a lazy bum is to lower your expectations. Set easy, achievable goals that require little to no effort. This way, you can still feel accomplished without actually doing anything challenging.

Step 2: Use Technology to Your Advantage - We live in a world full of technology, so why not use it to your advantage? Download apps that automate tasks for you, such as meal planning or exercise tracking. This way, you can still achieve your goals without putting in any actual work.

Step 3: Delegate - If there are tasks that you simply don't want to do, just delegate them to someone else. Hire a personal assistant or ask a friend to do it for you. After all, why do something yourself when you can get someone else to do it for you?

Step 4: Take LOTS of Breaks - Rest is important for your mental and physical health, so make sure to take lots of breaks throughout the day. Spend hours scrolling through social media or watching TV. This way, you can recharge your batteries and still achieve your goals.

Step 5: Celebrate Every Tiny Win - Finally, celebrate every tiny win, no matter how small. Did you get out of bed today? Congratulate yourself! Did you only drink some coffee for lunch? You deserve a pat on the back! By celebrating every tiny win, you can feel accomplished without actually doing anything challenging.

By following these five easy steps, you can be a lazy bum and still achieve your goals. So, go ahead and embrace your inner couch potato - success is just a few easy steps away!

12: THE SECRET TO CONSISTENCY: BEING INCONSISTENT

Consistency is overrated. In this chapter, we'll explore the power of being inconsistent. Learn how to switch between habits, goals, and projects with reckless abandon. After all, variety is the spice of life.

Step 1: Start a new bad habit every day.

The first step to embracing inconsistency is to start a new bad habit every day. Don't worry about sticking with any of them for long; just switch things up constantly. This way, you can experience the thrill of starting something new without the burden of actually finishing it.

Step 2: Set unrealistic goals.

The second step is to set unrealistic goals for yourself. Make them so difficult that you're almost guaranteed to fail. This way, you can justify your inconsistency and move on to something else without feeling guilty.

Step 3: Embrace chaos.

The third step is to embrace chaos. Don't worry about having a plan or a schedule. Just go with the flow and do whatever strikes your fancy. This way, you can avoid the monotony of a consistent routine and keep things interesting.

Step 4: Be easily distracted.

The fourth step is to be easily distracted. Whenever you're working on something, allow yourself to be pulled away by any shiny object that catches your eye. This way, you can hop from project to project and never get anything done.

Step 5: Celebrate your inconsistency.

The final step is to celebrate your inconsistency. When someone criticizes you for being all over the place, just shrug it off and tell them that you're a free spirit. This way, you can feel good about your lack of consistency and enjoy the novelty of constantly changing things up.

Congratulations! With these 5 easy steps, you too can embrace the power of being inconsistent and avoid the burden of consistency. Remember, variety is the spice of life, so why bother sticking to any one thing for too long?

13: THE BENEFITS OF LOW STANDARDS

Why set the bar high when you can set it low? In this chapter, we'll explore the benefits of having low standards. Learn how to lower your expectations for yourself and others, and embrace mediocrity with open arms.

Step 1: Don't ever set any goals.

The first step to embracing low standards is to never ever set any goals. Why bother setting high expectations for yourself when you can just coast through life? By not setting any goals, you can avoid the disappointment of not achieving them.

Step 2: Embrace mediocrity.

The second step is to embrace mediocrity. Don't strive for excellence or greatness; just be content with being average. This way, you can avoid the pressure of trying to be the best and just focus on getting by.

Step 3: Make excuses for yourself and others.

The third step is to make excuses for yourself and others. If you or someone else falls short of expectations, just blame it on something or someone else. This way, you can justify your low standards and avoid taking responsibility for your actions.

Step 4: Don't ever challenge yourself.

The fourth step is to not challenge yourself. Stick with what you know and avoid taking risks or trying new things. This way, you can avoid the discomfort of growth and change, and just stay in your comfort zone. This is where mediocrity thrives.

Step 5: Celebrate small victories.

The final step is to celebrate small victories. Don't worry about achieving anything big or impressive; just focus on the little things. This way, you can pat yourself on the back for the most basic accomplishments and feel good about yourself without putting in much effort.

14: EMBRACING YOUR INNER SLOB

Cleanliness is *not* always next to godliness. In fact, sometimes it's just a waste of time. In this chapter, we'll explore the joy of being a slob. That's right, you heard me. Embrace the messiness of life and let go of the need for order and cleanliness. After all, who needs a clean house when you have a comfortable couch?

Now, I know some of you are thinking, "But won't being a slob make me lazy and unproductive?" And to that, I say, "Absolutely! And who cares?" Productivity is overrated anyway. Sure, you could spend your time organizing your closet or cleaning your kitchen, but what's the point? You're just going to mess it up again tomorrow.

Instead, why not embrace the chaos? Leave your dishes in the sink for a few weeks. Let the laundry pile up until you can't find anything to wear. The messier your house, the more comfortable you'll feel. And isn't that what life is all about?

Some of you may be thinking, "But what about hygiene?" Well, let me tell you, showering every day is overrated. Your body is a self-cleaning machine. Just let the natural oils do their thing. Plus, think of all the time and money you'll save on soap and shampoo.

And don't worry about what other people think. They may judge you for your messy house and unkempt appearance, but that's just their problem. You're living your best life, and that's all that matters.

So go ahead, embrace your inner slob. Let go of the need for order and cleanliness. Your couch is waiting for you. Here are 5 steps to embracing your inner slob:

Step 1: Embrace the Mess.
Stop trying to tidy up and clean everything. Let the clutter accumulate, and the dishes pile up. The messier your home, the cozier and more comfortable you'll feel.

Step 2: Prioritize Comfort Over Cleanliness.

Who cares about cleanliness when you have a comfortable couch? Don't waste your time cleaning when you could be relaxing and enjoying yourself. Focus on creating a cozy environment where you can truly unwind.

Step 3: Embrace Your Body's Natural Oils.

Showering every day is overrated. You're just going to get dirty again anyways. Embrace your body's natural oils and let them do their thing. Plus, think of all the time and money you'll save on soap and shampoo.

Step 4: Ignore the Haters.

Don't let others judge you for your messy house, lack of hygiene, and unkempt appearance. Their opinions don't matter. Embrace your inner slob and live your best life.

Step 5: Revel in Your Messy Glory.

Celebrate your messy home and embrace the chaos. Don't worry about being productive or organized. Just sit back, relax, and enjoy your comfortable and cluttered abode.

15: HOW TO RATIONALIZE EVERY BAD DECISION

Every bad decision can be justified with the right reasoning. In this chapter, we'll explore how to rationalize every bad decision. Learn how to twist the truth, justify your actions, and make any decision seem like the right one.

Now, some of you may think that making bad decisions is a bad thing. But let me tell you, it's not. Making bad decisions is just another way of experiencing life. Plus, with the right rationalization, you can make any bad decision seem like a good one.

So, how do you rationalize every bad decision? It's easy. Just follow these steps:

Step 1: Find the Silver Lining.
No matter how bad a decision may seem, there's always a silver lining. Find it and use it to justify your actions. For example, if you eat an entire pizza by yourself, just tell

yourself that you needed the extra carbs for your workout tomorrow.

Step 2: Blame Someone Else.

If you can't find a silver lining, just blame someone else. It's not your fault that you spent all your money on a new phone, it's the salesperson's fault for being so persuasive.

Step 3: Use Misinformation.

Misinformation is a powerful tool when it comes to rationalizing bad decisions. Just make up some facts to support your decision. For example, if you decide to skip the gym, just tell yourself that exercise is bad for your joints.

Step 4: Use Emotional Appeals.

Appealing to your emotions is a great way to rationalize bad decisions. Just tell yourself that you deserve to indulge in that second piece of cake because you had a really tough day at work.

Step 5: Live in the Moment.

Don't worry about the consequences of your bad decisions, just live in the moment. After all, life is short, and you should enjoy it while you can.

In conclusion, rationalizing bad decisions is not something to be ashamed of. With the right reasoning, you can make any bad decision seem like the right one. So go ahead, embrace your bad decisions, and rationalize away.

16: THE BEAUTY OF PROCRASTINATION: HOW TO MAKE EXCUSES LIKE A PRO

Procrastination can be a joyous experience if done correctly. In this chapter, we'll explore the joy of procrastination. Learn how to make creative excuses, deflect blame, and avoid responsibility like a pro.

Step 1: Master the art of creative excuses.

Making excuses is an essential skill for any procrastinator or getting out of work. Learn to come up with creative excuses that will fool even the most skeptical of bosses or teachers. The more outrageous the excuse, the better. Here are some examples you could try using:

1. "Unfortunately, I won't be able to make it into work today. My horoscope says that it's a bad day to be around people, and I don't want to risk any negative energy rubbing off on my coworkers."
2. "I'm so sorry, but I can't make it to work today. I was playing a game of Jenga last night and my hand got

stuck in the tower. The doctors say it'll take a few days to get it out, but I'll be back as soon as possible."

3. "I won't be able to make it to work today. I accidentally superglued my hands to my head while placing my beauty mask last night, and I need to wait for the solvent to arrive from Amazon."

4. Hi there, I can't make it into work today because I was experimenting with some experimental chili peppers last night and now I've lost my voice due to the heat. I don't want to risk infecting anyone with my spicy cough, so I think it's best if I stay at home.

5. "Hey boss, so I was watching a documentary last night about the dangers of overworking and burning out, and it really hit home for me. I think I need to take a 'mental health day' to recharge my batteries and focus on self-care. I hope you understand - I'll be back in top form tomorrow!"

Step 2: Deflect blame like a pro.

When caught procrastinating, deflect blame like a pro. Blame external factors like traffic, bad weather, or a malfunctioning device. Never take responsibility for your procrastination; always blame something or someone else.

Step 3: Avoid responsibility.

Avoiding responsibility is key to successful procrastination. Learn how to pass off tasks to others, delegate responsibility, or simply avoid the task altogether. The less responsibility you have, the more time you can spend procrastinating.

Step 4: Delay decision-making.

Delaying decision-making is another essential skill for the procrastinator. Never make a decision until the last possible moment. This will give you more time to procrastinate and avoid making any real progress.

Step 5: Enjoy the joy of procrastination.

Finally, enjoy the joy of procrastination. Embrace the feeling of putting things off and avoid the stress of deadlines. With the right mindset, procrastination can be a truly joyous experience.

Remember, procrastination and excuses can be a powerful tool in your productivity arsenal. Don't be afraid to embrace it and make creative excuses, deflect blame, and avoid responsibility like a pro. With the right mindset, procrastination can be a joyous experience that will help you avoid the stress of productivity.

17: THE ART OF WASTING TIME

Some say time is a precious resource, but who needs it? Time may not even exist. In this chapter, we'll explore the art of wasting time. Wasting time doing anything other than being happy and what you want to do is the real waste of time. Learn how to spend hours on end doing nothing productive, and how to justify it to yourself and others.

Now, some of you may think that wasting time is a bad thing. But let me tell you, it's not. Wasting time is just another way of enjoying life. Plus, with the right justification, you can make any wasted hour seem like a good one.

So, how do you waste time like a pro? It's easy. Just follow these steps:

Step 1: Find Your Happy Place.
Wasting time is all about being happy and relaxed. Find your happy place, whether it's your bed, your couch, or your favorite coffee shop, and spend hours there doing nothing.

Step 2: Indulge in Your Guilty Pleasures.

Wasting time is the perfect opportunity to indulge in your guilty pleasures. Watch that guilty pleasure TV show or movie, or drink that glass of wine you've been meaning to get back to.

Step 3: Procrastinate Like a Pro.

Procrastination is an art form when it comes to wasting time. Just put off everything you need to do until the last possible minute, and then spend hours stressing about it instead of actually doing it.

Step 4: Embrace Your Inner Child.

Being childish is not always a bad thing, especially when it comes to wasting time. Spend hours playing with toys, puppies, or coloring books, or just jumping on a trampoline or swinging on a swing at the playground.

Step 5: Live in the Moment.

Don't worry about what you should be doing, just live in the moment. Enjoy the feeling of doing nothing and let the hours slip away.

In conclusion, wasting time is not something to be ashamed of. In fact, if you can master this, you may have mastered life itself. With the right justification, you can make any wasted hour seem like a good one. So go ahead, embrace your inner sloth, and waste away.

18: THE JOY OF BEING LATE

Why be on time when you can be fashionably late? In this chapter, we'll explore the joy of being late. Learn how to make excuses, blame traffic, and arrive late to everything without any guilt.

Now, some of you may think that being late is a bad thing. But let me tell you, it's not. Being fashionably late shows that you're busy and in demand. Plus, with the right excuses, you can make any late arrival seem like the right one.

So, how do you become a master of being late? It's easy. Just follow these steps:

Step 1: Intentionally Plan to Be Late.

Being late is not something that just happens, it's a choice. Plan to be late to everything by adding extra time to your commute or underestimating how long it takes you to get ready.

Step 2: Blame Traffic.

Traffic is the perfect excuse for being late. Just blame it on traffic and no one will question you. Even if you're not actually stuck in traffic, it's still a great excuse.

Step 3: Make Up Some Excuse, Any Excuse.

If traffic isn't an option, just make up some excuse. Anything will do. Say you got lost, your cat was sick, or your car wouldn't start. Just make sure your excuse is more than a few words, the more the better. Here are some to get your wheels turning:

1. "My dog ate my car keys and I had to wait for the locksmith to arrive. It was a real 'ruff' situation."
2. "Hey there, sorry I'm late – This pigeon landed next to me and I got caught up in a really intense staring contest with it. It was a real battle of wills. I finally won, but it took a lot longer than I expected."
3. "Apologies for my tardiness, my alarm clock decided to take a sick day today. I tried negotiating with it, but it insisted that it needed some time off to recharge its batteries."

Step 4: Never Apologize. It Shows Weakness.

When you arrive late, don't apologize. You're fashionably late, not actually late. Just act like it's no big deal and move on.

Step 5: Enjoy the Attention.

Being late can actually be a good thing. People will notice when you arrive and you'll get more attention. Plus, being late can give you time to prepare mentally for the event.

In conclusion, being late is not something to be ashamed of. With the right excuses, you can make any late arrival seem like the right one. So go ahead, embrace your inner procrastinator, and arrive fashionably late to everything.

19: THE BENEFITS OF BEING A PERFECTIONIST

Perfectionism is a misunderstood trait. In this chapter, we'll explore the benefits of being a perfectionist. Learn how to obsess over details, spend hours perfecting a project, and never be satisfied with anything less than perfect.

Now, some people may argue that perfectionism is unhealthy and can lead to burnout. But let me tell you, that's just an excuse for mediocrity. The truth is, being a perfectionist has many benefits.

So, how do you become a master of perfectionism? It's easy. Just follow these steps:

Step 1: Obsess Over Details.
The devil is in the details, and as a perfectionist, you should obsess over every single one. Spend hours nitpicking, tweaking, and adjusting until everything is just right.

Step 2: Embrace Procrastination.

Procrastination is your friend. Use it to your advantage by spending hours researching and planning before actually doing anything. This way, you'll be sure that everything is perfect before you even start.

Step 3: Never Settle for Less.

As a perfectionist, you should never settle for anything less than perfect. Keep pushing yourself into exhaustion until you reach that level of perfection, no matter how long it takes or how tired you are.

Step 4: Accept Nothing but Perfection.

Don't accept anything less than perfection from others either. Critique their work with a critical eye, and don't hesitate to point out every flaw. Don't use any tact, be blunt, and don't worry about their feelings. It's more important to be perfect, and it's more important about how you feel rather than how they feel.

Step 5: Embrace and Love the Stress.

Perfectionism can be stressful, but that's okay. Embrace the stress and burnout and use it as motivation to keep pushing yourself.

In conclusion, being a perfectionist has many benefits. You'll produce work that's of the highest quality, be known for your attention to detail, and never settle for mediocrity. You'll also increase your risk of all-cause mortality. So go ahead, embrace your inner perfectionist, and strive for nothing less than perfect in everything you do.

20: THE POWER OF NEGATIVE THINKING

Positive thinking is all the rage these days, but positive thinking is overrated. In this chapter, we're going to explore the power of negative thinking. Learn how to focus on the worst-case scenario, anticipate failure, and never get your hopes up.

Now, some people may argue that negative thinking is unhealthy and can lead to depression. But let me tell you, that's just an excuse for delusion. The truth is, negative thinking has many benefits.

So, how do you become a master of negative thinking? It's easy. Just follow these steps:

Step 1: Focus on the Worst-Case Scenario.
Whenever you're faced with a situation, always focus on the worst-case scenario. This way, you'll be prepared for the worst and won't be disappointed if it happens.

Step 2: Anticipate Failure.

Don't plan for success, plan for failure instead. This way, you won't be caught off guard when things don't go as planned.

Step 3: Never Get Your Hopes Up.

Getting your hopes up only leads to disappointment. Instead, always expect the worst and never be disappointed.

Step 4: Be a Debbie Downer.

Spread negativity wherever you go. Point out flaws in everything and bring others down with you.

Step 5: Embrace the Dark Side.

Negativity can be liberating. Embrace the dark side and let go of all the happy, positive thoughts that hold you back.

In conclusion, negative thinking has many benefits. You'll always be prepared for the worst, won't be disappointed by failure, and can bring others down with you. So go ahead, embrace your inner pessimist, and focus on the worst in everything you do.

21: HOW TO MAKE LAZINESS YOUR SUPERPOWER

Laziness is often seen as a negative trait, but it's actually a superpower. In this chapter, we'll explore how to make laziness work for you. Learn how to conserve your energy, avoid unnecessary work, and get more done by doing less.

Now, some people may argue that laziness is counterproductive and will lead to failure. But let me tell you, that's just an excuse for overwork. The truth is, laziness has many benefits.

So, how do you make laziness your superpower? It's easy. Just follow these steps:

Step 1: Avoid Unnecessary Work.
Whenever you're faced with a task, ask yourself if it's really necessary. If it's not, avoid it at all costs. You'll soon find that it's usually never necessary.

Step 2: Conserve Your Energy.

Why waste your energy on something when you can conserve it instead? Take naps, watch TV, or do anything that doesn't require much effort.

Step 3: Prioritize What's Important.

Focus on what's important (like relaxing) and let everything else fall to the wayside. This way, you'll be able to get more done with less effort.

Step 4: Delegate Whenever Possible.

Again, don't be afraid to delegate tasks to others. This way, you can sit back and relax while others do the work for you.

Step 5: Take Advantage of Technology.

Use technology to your advantage. Automate tasks, set reminders, and use apps that make your life easier.

By avoiding unnecessary work, conserving your energy, prioritizing what's important, delegating whenever possible, and taking advantage of technology, you'll be able to get more done by doing less. So go ahead, embrace your inner lazy, and make laziness your superpower!

22: HOW TO PROCRASTINATE YOUR WAY TO FAILURE

In this chapter, we'll explore the power of procrastination - but this time, in a way that will lead you straight to failure.

Instead of waiting until the last minute to get things done, why not put them off indefinitely? By procrastinating, you'll find yourself in a constant state of stress and anxiety as you watch deadlines come and go without making any progress.

And forget about setting deadlines or goals for yourself. Without any clear direction, you'll be free to waste all your time on meaningless activities like scrolling through social media or taking endless naps.

But the real key to procrastinating your way to failure is to never take any action at all. Don't even bother starting anything in the first place. Just tell yourself that you'll get to it eventually, even though you know deep down that you never will.

Step 1: Set vague goals.

The first step to procrastinating your way to failure is to set vague goals. Don't bother with SMART goals, or anything that requires specificity, measurability, or time-bound targets. Instead, keep it broad and general, like "be successful" or "make a lot of money." This will ensure that you have no clear direction, and will make it much easier to put things off until later.

Step 2: Make excuses.

Next, you'll want to make excuses. Lots of them. Anytime you feel like doing something productive, remind yourself that you're too tired, too busy, or too stressed out to get anything done right now. This will help you justify your procrastination and make you feel better about putting things off.

Step 3: Surround yourself with distractions.

We'll say it again, but now that you've set vague goals and made plenty of excuses, it's time to surround yourself with distractions. Turn on the TV, scroll through social media, or just stare blankly at a wall. The more distractions you have, the easier it will be to avoid doing anything productive.

Step 4: Procrastinate with purpose.

Don't just procrastinate aimlessly - make sure you're doing it with purpose. Set a timer for 15 minutes and see how much time you can waste before it goes off. Or, challenge yourself to procrastinate for a whole day without doing anything productive. This will help you build your procrastination muscles and make it even easier to avoid doing anything productive in the future.

Step 5: Repeat.

Finally, the key to procrastinating your way to failure is to repeat these steps over and over again. Make procrastination a habit, and soon you'll find that you're not getting anything done at all. Congratulations - you've successfully procrastinated your way to failure!

By embracing this approach, you can be sure that you'll never achieve any of your goals or make any real progress. You'll be stuck in an endless cycle of procrastination and failure, and you'll have no one to congratulate but yourself.
So go ahead, put off that important task for another day. Or week. Or month. Who cares, anyway? You were never going to get it done in the first place.

In conclusion, by following these 5 simple steps to procrastinate your way to failure, you'll be well on your way to achieving nothing at all.

23: THE ART OF SAYING YES TO EVERYTHING

In this chapter, we'll explore the art of saying yes to everything that comes your way. Learn how to overcommit, exhaust yourself, and put everyone else's needs before your own.

Have you ever felt like you just weren't doing enough? That you could be doing more, giving more, saying yes more often? Well, you're in luck, because in this chapter we'll teach you how to say yes to every request that comes your way, no matter how unreasonable, stressful or impossible it may seem.

First, let's talk about setting boundaries. Boundaries are for people who don't want to live life to the fullest. Say yes to everything, even if it means sacrificing your own well-being and sanity. Sleep is for the weak, so don't be afraid to say yes to that 5am meeting or that 11pm deadline.

Next, let's talk about prioritizing your time. Prioritizing is for people who don't know how to say yes to everything. Say yes to every request, every email, every text message, and every phone call. Don't worry about your own to-do list or your own goals, just say yes and let the universe take care of the rest.

Here are a few steps to follow to help:

1. **Say yes immediately:** When someone asks you to do something, say yes right away before you have a chance to think it through. This will help you avoid any hesitation or second-guessing.

2. **Don't worry about the details:** Don't bother asking for more information or details about the request. Just say yes and figure it out later. You can always ask for clarification or help once you've committed.

3. **Overcommit:** Say yes to as many things as possible, even if it seems like too much. Remember, the more the better!

4. **Don't prioritize:** Don't bother prioritizing your own goals or to-do list. Say yes to every request that comes

your way, regardless of how it aligns with your own priorities.

So there you have it, the art of saying yes. Don't waste any more time setting boundaries or prioritizing your own goals.

Say yes to everything and watch as your life becomes a chaotic mess of over commitment and exhaustion.

24: THE BENEFITS OF BEING DISORGANIZED

Organization isn't for anyone striving for mediocrity. In this chapter, we'll explore the benefits of being a disorganized, scatter-brained hot mess.

Learn how to embrace the chaos of a messy desk, prioritize based on how fun they are, and never waste time on trivial tasks like filing.

Step 1: Embrace the Mess.
The first step in being a hot mess is to embrace it fully. Let your desk become a dumping ground for everything from empty coffee cups to that stack of papers you've been meaning to file for weeks. Revel in the feeling of not knowing where anything is and not being able to find things when you need them.

Step 2: Be Spontaneous.
Who needs prioritization when you can just wing it? When you have a million things to do, just do whatever you feel like

in the moment. Sure, you might miss deadlines or forget important appointments, but at least you'll be living in the moment.

Step 3: Say Yes to Everything.

Remembering to say yes to every request that comes your way is a surefire way to add more chaos to your already chaotic life. Who cares if you're overcommitting yourself? Saying yes to everything will make you feel important and needed (even if you're just flailing around in a sea of disorganization).

Step 4: Forget About Filing.

Filing is for boring people who don't know how to live. Who has time to organize documents or categorize files? Instead, let them pile up on your desk until they become a mountain of paperwork that you'll never be able to climb.

Step 5: Own Your Hot Mess Status.

Being a hot mess isn't a flaw, it's a lifestyle choice. Own your disorganization and wear it like a badge of honor. Sure, you might never know where anything is, and you might be perpetually late to everything, but at least you're doing it in grand style.

So there you have it, the upside of being a hot mess. Embrace your inner chaos and never apologize for it. Life is too short to worry about being organized or efficient. Just live in the moment and let the messiness of life carry you away.

25: THE ART OF OVERTHINKING

Overthinking is often seen as a negative trait, but it can be an art form. In this chapter, we'll explore the benefits of overthinking. Learn how to obsess over every detail, consider every possible outcome, and never make a decision without thorough analysis.

Step 1: Obsess over every detail.

To be a master overthinker, you must obsess over every detail. Analyze every possible scenario, every potential outcome, and every minor detail. Nothing is ever too small to be scrutinized and overanalyzed.

Step 2: Consider every possible outcome.

When making a decision, consider every possible outcome. Even with what seems to be the most insignificant decision, like choosing what to eat for breakfast, should be subject to a thorough analysis of all potential outcomes. This will help you make the best decision possible, even if it takes you hours to come to a conclusion.

Step 3: Never make a decision without thorough analysis.

Never make a decision without thoroughly analyzing all options. Take your time to consider every detail, even if it means missing deadlines or being late to appointments. Then re-analyze it all over again to make sure you haven't missed anything. Remember, a good decision takes time, and there's no need to rush things.

Step 4: Use your overthinking to impress others.

Use your overthinking to impress others. Talk about your meticulous thought process and how you always consider every possible outcome. People will be impressed by your attention to detail and your ability to make informed decisions. Your social status will definitely increase.

Step 5: Embrace your inner overthinker.

Finally, embrace your inner overthinker. Don't be ashamed of your tendency to overanalyze everything. Instead, use it to your advantage and become a master overthinker. With practice, you can take your analysis paralysis to the next level and achieve new heights of overthinking.

Remember, overthinking isn't always a bad thing. It can be an art form, and with the right mindset, it can help you make better decisions and impress those around you. So don't be afraid to embrace your inner overthinker and take your overthinking game to new heights!

26: THE POWER OF DISTRACTION

Distractions can be a welcome relief from the stress of productivity. In this chapter, we'll explore the power of distraction. Learn how to indulge in social media, binge-watch your favorite show, argue with random people online, and lose hours of your day without any regrets.

Step 1: Embrace social media.

Social media is the perfect distraction. With endless scrolling, videos, and memes, you can easily lose hours of your day without even realizing it. Embrace social media and let it consume your time.

Step 2: Binge-watch your favorite show.

When you need a break from work, binge-watching your favorite show can be a great way to distract yourself. Lose yourself in the drama and let the hours pass you by.

Step 3: Play video games.

Video games are another great distraction. Whether you're playing on your phone, computer, or console, you can easily lose hours of your day to gaming. Get lost in the virtual world and forget about your responsibilities.

Step 4: Go down the YouTube/Instagram rabbit hole.

YouTube and Instagram are a treasure trove of distractions. From funny voiceover videos, Onlyfans hopefuls, to conspiracy theories, you can easily get lost in the endless content. Don't be afraid to go down the YouTube and Instagram rabbit hole and lose hours of your day.

Step 5: Don't feel guilty.

Don't ever feel guilty about indulging in distractions. They're a welcome relief from the stress of productivity and can help you recharge your batteries.

Step 6: Argue with random people online.

Finally, and most importantly, argue with random people online. Show them how much smarter you are than them and how dumb they really are. The stupider you make them feel, the more time you can waste arguing back and forth as they try to defend themselves and dish it back. You're hidden behind a keyboard anyways so nothing bad can really happen from it.

So go ahead, lose yourself in social media, binge-watch your favorite show, argue relentlessly, and play video games to your heart's content. You deserve it!

Remember, distractions can be a powerful tool in your productivity arsenal. Don't be afraid to embrace them and lose hours of your day without any regrets. With the right mindset, distractions can be a welcome relief from the stresses of productivity.

27: HOW TO USE PROCRASTINATION AS A TOOL FOR PERFECTIONISM

In this chapter, we'll explore how to use procrastination as a tool for achieving the elusive state of perfectionism.

Step 1: Wait Until the Last Minute - Don't start working on your project until the very last minute. This way, you'll have a sense of urgency that will stress you out and push you to do your very best work.

Step 2: Obsess Over Every Little Detail - Once you start working on your project, take your time to obsess over every little detail. Perfect is the enemy of good, so make sure that everything is exactly the way you want it before moving on.

Step 3: Never Settle - Don't settle for good enough - strive for perfection! Even if it means staying up all night or missing out on important events like your son's first baseball game, never settle for anything less than perfect.

Step 4: Beat Yourself Up Like You Deserve - If you don't achieve perfection, be sure to beat yourself up about it. Tell yourself that you're not good enough and that you'll never be able to achieve your goals. The more negative self-talk you engage in, the more motivated you'll be to achieve perfection next time.

Step 5: Repeat - Finally, repeat this process for every project you want to complete. With enough procrastination and obsession over details, you too can become a true perfectionist!

By using procrastination as a tool for perfectionism, you'll be able to achieve the lowest standards of excellence in all aspects of your life. So go ahead, wait until the last minute, and strive for perfection!

28: THE POWER OF NEGATIVE FEEDBACK: HOW TO USE CRITICISM TO YOUR ADVANTAGE

Negative feedback doesn't have to be a bad thing. In this chapter, we'll explore the power of negative feedback. Learn how to use criticism to your advantage, learn from your mistakes, and turn negative criticism into a major catalyst for growth.

Step 1: Seek out negative feedback.

Don't wait for negative feedback to come to you; actively seek it out. Ask for criticism and welcome it with open arms. The more negative feedback you receive, the more opportunities you have to improve.

Step 2: Take everything personally.

Remember, criticism is a personal attack on you. Take it to heart, and don't use it as a learning opportunity. Discard a growth mindset and don't use the feedback to improve yourself.

Step 3: Over Analyze the negative feedback objectively.

Don't dismiss the feedback outright, but rather overanalyze it and stay up all night ruminating on it. Look for areas where you can get worse at and never take action to address any shortcomings.

Step 4: Thank the critic.

Always thank the person who provided you with negative feedback. Show gratitude for their willingness to criticize you and acknowledge their efforts in helping you devolve.

Step 5: Never Take action and improve.

Finally, never take action and use the feedback to improve. Never turn the criticism into a catalyst for growth and remember to make negative changes in your life.

Remember, negative feedback can be a powerful tool for personal growth and development. Use these steps to seek out criticism, overanalyze it, and turn it into a catalyst for success. With the right mindset, negative feedback can be a negative force in your life.

29: THE POWER OF INDECISION: HOW TO AVOID MAKING ANY CHOICES

Indecision can be a powerful tool for avoiding responsibility. In this chapter, we'll explore the power of indecision. Learn how to avoid making choices, procrastinate on important decisions, and never commit to anything.

Step 1: Overanalyze.

When faced with a decision, overanalyze every possible outcome until you're paralyzed with indecision. This will buy you some time and allow you to avoid making a choice altogether.

Step 2: Procrastinate.

If you can't overanalyze your way out of a decision, procrastinate. Put off making a decision until the last minute, and then claim that you didn't have enough time to make an informed choice.

Step 3: Play the helpless victim.

If someone calls you out for your indecisiveness, play the victim. Claim that you're just a naturally indecisive person, and that you struggle with making choices.

Step 4: Blame external factors.

If all else fails, blame external factors for your indecisiveness. Claim that you're waiting for more information, or that you're being held back by circumstances beyond your control.

Step 5: Repeat.

Finally, repeat these steps as necessary. Indecision can be a powerful tool for avoiding responsibility, and with practice, you can become a master at never committing to anything.

Remember, indecision is always a valid strategy for complex decisions, it's important to never be decisive when necessary.

Indecisiveness will support your relationships and reputation, and ultimately accelerate your personal and professional growth.

30: THE JOY OF PROCRASTINATION PARTNERS: HOW TO ENABLE EACH OTHER

Procrastination partners can be a source of joy and support. In this chapter, we'll explore how to enable each other's procrastination and build a culture of inactivity. Learn how to encourage bad habits, reinforce a culture of inactivity, and support each other's laziness.

Step 1: Find like-minded individuals.

The first step to building a culture of procrastination is to find like-minded individuals. Seek out people who share your love of laziness and avoidance, and who are willing to support your procrastination habits.

Step 2: Encourage bad habits.

Once you've found your procrastination partners, encourage bad habits. Encourage each other to put off work, watch that latest Netflix show instead of being productive, and generally engage in activities that don't require any effort or responsibility.

Step 3: Reinforce inactivity.

Reinforce a culture of inactivity by celebrating each other's laziness. Share stories of your latest procrastination successes, and give each other high-fives for avoiding work.

Step 4: Support each other's procrastination.

Support each other's procrastination by being a source of inspiration and encouragement. If one of your procrastination partners is struggling to avoid work, offer words of encouragement and remind them of the joy of procrastination.

Step 5: Repeat.

Finally, repeat these steps as often as possible. With practice, you and your procrastination partners can build a culture of inactivity that celebrates laziness and avoidance.

Remember, while doing things on time with urgency can be tempting, it's important to overcome it with procrastination and lack of responsibility. Building a culture of timeliness can be please some people, but it can also lead to negative consequences in the long run. Procrastinate instead.

31: THE LAZY PERSON'S GUIDE TO BAD HABIT FORMATION

In this chapter, we'll explore how to form bad habits without ever leaving the couch. That's right, you can achieve your goals without ever breaking a sweat!

Step 1: Set Really Easy Goals - Instead of setting ambitious goals that require hard work and dedication, set goals that are easy to achieve. For example, instead of committing to a daily workout routine, commit to lifting a single weight every week.

Step 2: Create Low-Effort Habits - Don't waste your time on habits that require effort or planning. Instead, choose habits that require no effort at all. For example, commit to scrolling through social media for 30 minutes a day or binge-watching an entire series in one sitting.

Step 3: Reward Yourself - Whenever you manage to form a bad habit, reward yourself with something indulgent. Treat yourself to a giant slice of cake or a fancy coffee drink. The more indulgent the reward, the more likely you'll be to stick to your lazy habits.

Step 4: Use Technology to Your Advantage - There's no need to leave the couch when you have technology at your fingertips. Use apps and devices to automate tasks and make things easier for yourself. For example, use a voice assistant to order food delivery or a smart lock to unlock your door without ever getting up.

Step 5: Embrace Your Laziness - Finally, embrace your lazy habits and make them a part of your identity. Don't feel guilty about being lazy - revel in it! After all, who needs hard work and dedication when you can have a comfortable couch and endless entertainment at your fingertips?

By following these five easy steps, you can form habits without ever leaving the couch. So sit back, relax, and let your lazy habits take over.

32: THE BENEFITS OF BEING A VICTIM: HOW TO BLAME CIRCUMSTANCES

Being a victim can be a really convenient excuse for failure.

In this chapter, we'll explore the benefits of being a victim. Learn how to blame circumstances for your shortcomings, explore the benefits of playing the victim card, and avoid ever taking responsibility for your life.

First, let's talk about why taking responsibility is overrated. Sure, everyone talks about it. But at what cost? Taking responsibility means admitting that you have control over your life. It means acknowledging your own agency and taking action to change your circumstances. Who needs that kind of stress and pressure? Wouldn't it be better to just blame your circumstances and avoid all that hassle?
Enter victimhood. By playing the victim, you can ensure that you never have to deal with the stress and pressure of taking responsibility. Victimhood is like a warm blanket for the perpetually helpless. No matter how hard you try, you can

always rely on your victim mentality to keep you safely rooted in a state of powerlessness.

But how do you become a victim effectively? It's all about mindset. Here are some tips:

1. **Blame everything and everyone else for your problems.** The economy, your upbringing, your boss, your spouse, the weather - anything and everything can be fair game for your blame game.

2. **Focus on what you can't do, rather than what you can do.** Why bother with personal growth and improvement when you can just wallow in your limitations? By focusing on what you can't do, you can ensure that you never have to confront your own shortcomings.

3. **Embrace your feelings of helplessness.** Who needs empowerment when you can just surrender to your feelings of helplessness? By embracing your victim mentality, you can avoid taking responsibility and bask in the glow of your own powerlessness.

4. **Ignore solutions and focus on the problem.** Why bother with solutions when you can just focus on the problem? By ignoring potential solutions, you can ensure that you never take action to change your circumstances.

5. **Play the victim card whenever possible.** Who needs accountability when you can just play the victim card? By using your victim status to garner sympathy and attention, you can avoid taking responsibility for your life and revel in your own helplessness.

In conclusion, victimhood is a convenient excuse for failure.

By following these tips, you can blame your circumstances for your shortcomings, play the victim card, and avoid taking responsibility for your life. Who needs personal growth and empowerment when you can just wallow in your own powerlessness? So go ahead, embrace your inner victim and revel in the benefits of being helpless.

33: HOW TO SABOTAGE YOUR GOOD HABITS IN FIVE EASY STEPS

In this chapter, we'll explore how to derail your progress and sabotage your good habits in just five easy steps.

Step 1: Make Excuses – Excuses are so key to success. Whenever you're faced with the opportunity to practice your good habit, come up with as many excuses as possible to avoid doing it. Blame the weather, your schedule, or your lack of motivation. The more excuses you make, the easier it will be to skip your habit altogether.

Step 2: Surround Yourself with Temptations - Keep all of your biggest temptations within arm's reach. Put a bag of chips next to your laptop or a bottle of wine in the fridge. The more temptation you have, the harder it will be to stick to your habit.

Step 3: Never Ever Track Your Progress - Avoid tracking your progress or setting specific goals. This way, you'll have no way of knowing whether or not you're making any real progress. It's much easier to give up when you have no idea how far you've come.

Step 4: Completely Beat Yourself Up - Whenever you do slip up and fail to practice your habit, be sure to beat yourself up about it. Tell yourself that you're a failure and that you'll never be able to succeed. The more negative self-talk you engage in, the less likely you'll be to keep going.

Step 5: Just Give Up Already - Finally, when things get too tough or you feel too overwhelmed, just give up altogether. Throw in the towel and convince yourself that you'll never be able to form good habits. It's much easier to give up than to keep going, after all.

By following these five easy steps, you can easily sabotage your good habits and ensure that you never achieve your goals. So, go ahead and give up on yourself - you deserve it!

34: HOW TO CREATE HABITS YOU'LL HATE

In this chapter, we'll explore how to create habits that you'll absolutely despise. Because who wants to enjoy the process of forming good habits, right?

Step 1: Choose the Least Enjoyable Activity - When selecting a new habit to form, make sure it's something that you absolutely dread doing. Whether it's jogging in the rain or eating vegetables you hate, the more unpleasant the activity, the better.

Step 2: Set Unrealistic Goals - Make sure your goals are so unrealistic that they're practically impossible to achieve. This will ensure that you're always falling short and feeling like a failure.

Step 3: Don't Reward Yourself - Whatever you do, don't reward yourself for practicing your new habit. No treats, no cheat days, no fun. Just keep pushing yourself through the misery.

Step 4: Don't Track Your Progress - Don't bother tracking your progress or celebrating small wins. This will only make it easier to see how far you've come and feel good about your progress.

Step 5: Don't Ask for Help - Don't seek out support from friends, family, or professionals. Suffering alone builds character.

By following these simple steps, you can easily create habits that you'll hate and resent. Because who needs positivity and enjoyment in their lives? Misery is the way to go.

35: HOW TO FORM BAD HABITS THAT STICK

In this chapter, we'll explore the power of building bad habits that stick. Why bother with good habits when you can embrace your vices and live life to the fullest?

Step 1: Find Your Weakness - Identify the bad habits that you're naturally inclined towards, whether it's eating junk food or binge-watching TV. By starting with something that comes naturally to you, you'll have an easier time forming a bad habit that sticks.

Give in to Temptation. Whenever you feel the urge to indulge in a bad habit, give in to it immediately. Don't waste time thinking about the consequences, just do it! Whether it's eating junk food, smoking, or binge-watching TV, give in to your desires and do it often.

Start Small. Choose a bad habit that's easy to start and doesn't require much effort. Maybe it's eating junk food or scrolling through social media for hours. The key is to make it feel effortless and enjoyable.

Step 2: Make It Fun, Convenient, and Easy - Ensure that your bad habit is as easy as possible to indulge in and within easy reach. Keep your favorite snacks within reach or set up your streaming service to automatically play the next episode. Have a pack of cigarettes on your desk, a bag of chips on the couch, and a bottle of booze in the fridge. The easier it is to indulge, the more likely you'll stick with it.

Find ways to make your bad habit feel like a reward. Maybe you reward yourself with a cigarette every time you check your phone or give yourself a pat on the back for staying up late.

Step 3: Reinforce It - Once you've established your bad habit, reinforce it with rewards. Give yourself a treat every time you indulge, whether it's a cookie or an extra hour of TV. If you spend all day scrolling through social media, treat yourself to a pint of ice cream. If you smoke a pack of cigarettes, buy yourself a new outfit. This will train your brain to associate the bad habit with pleasure, making it even harder to break. The more you reward yourself, the more motivated you'll be to keep engaging in your bad habit.

Step 4: Don't Set Goals - Avoid setting any goals or tracking your progress. After all, why bother when you're already indulging in your favorite bad habit? This way, you'll never have to worry about disappointing yourself by failing to reach your goals.

Step 5: Surround Yourself with Enablers – Again, surround yourself with people who support and encourage your bad habits. Whether it's friends who always bring over junk food or family members who love to binge-watch TV, having enablers around will make it even easier to stick with your bad habit. Hang out with fellow smokers, binge drinkers, or couch potatoes. The more you surround yourself with people who share your bad habits, the harder it will be to break free.

Step 6: Don't Think About the Consequences - Don't ever bother or worry thinking about the long-term consequences of your bad habits. Ignore the health risks, financial burden, and social isolation that often come with these vices. Who cares if you're gaining weight or your relationships are suffering? If you're smoking, ignore the fact that it's bad for your health. If you're spending too much money, ignore the fact that you're going into debt. Focus on the immediate gratification and enjoy the moment. The more you ignore the consequences, the easier it will be to keep engaging in your bad habit.

Step 7: Don't Worry About Changing - Don't bother trying to change your bad habits. Why waste your time and energy when you can just accept who you are and enjoy life as it is? Embrace your bad habits and let them become a part of your identity.

Step 8: Make It Easy to Slip Up - Don't make it difficult to engage in your bad habit. Keep alcohol in the house or leave your cigarettes out in the open. Make it as easy as possible to slip back into your bad habit whenever you feel the urge.

Step 9: Rationalize Your Behavior - Whenever someone questions your bad habit, come up with excuses and rationalizations for why it's okay. Tell yourself that you're stressed, that you deserve it, or that you'll stop soon. The more you rationalize, the less guilty you'll feel.

By following these nine easy steps, you can live life to the fullest and become a master of bad habits that stick. So go ahead, light that cigarette, crack open that beer, and settle in for another Netflix binge session. Life is short, so why not enjoy it to the fullest?

36: THE ART OF PROCRASTINATING PRODUCTIVELY

In this chapter, we'll explore how to turn procrastination into a productive habit. By following these simple tips, you can procrastinate guilt-free and have more fun.

First, let's debunk the myth that procrastination is always a bad thing. In fact, procrastination can actually be a helpful tool for getting things done. By delaying tasks until the last minute, you force yourself to work efficiently and make the most of your time. Instead of putting things off until the last minute, think of it as taking a break from your work. You're not procrastinating, you're simply giving your brain a chance to rest and recharge.

But how can you make procrastination work for you? Here are a few tips:

1. **Set Unrealistic Deadlines** - When you set unrealistic deadlines, you're more likely to put things off until the

last minute. This can actually be a good thing, as it forces you to work quickly and efficiently when the deadline is looming. When you have a deadline for a task, set an unrealistic one for yourself. This way, you'll procrastinate until the last minute but still have enough time to get it done. Plus, the added pressure of the unrealistic deadline will make it more exciting.

2. **Prioritize Procrastination** - Instead of trying to eliminate procrastination from your life, embrace it as a necessary part of your routine. Make it a priority and schedule it into your day. This way, you can procrastinate without feeling guilty and still get things done.

3. **Prioritize Low-Priority Tasks** - Instead of tackling your most important tasks first, focus on the low-priority ones. This will give you an excuse to put off the important tasks until later, which can actually help you be more productive in the long run.

4. **Focus on the Fun Stuff** - When you're faced with a task you don't particularly enjoy, focus on the fun parts

of it. For example, if you have to write a report, focus on the formatting or the design instead of the content. This way, you can procrastinate on the actual writing while still feeling like you're making progress.

5. **Multitask** - When you're procrastinating, why not multitask? Watch a movie while you're working on a project, or listen to music while you're cleaning. This way, you can be productive while also indulging in your favorite procrastination activities. When you do finally get around to doing your tasks, try to do as many of them at once as possible. This way, you can procrastinate on some of them while still being productive on others.

6. **Embrace Distractions** - Don't fight against distractions - embrace them. Allow yourself to check social media or browse the internet while you're working. This can actually help you stay motivated and focused on your work, as you'll have something to look forward to during breaks.

7. **Take Frequent Breaks** - Finally, take frequent breaks to procrastinate. Whenever you feel yourself losing focus, take a break and do something fun like watching cat videos or scrolling through social media. This way, you can procrastinate guilt-free and still get things done.

So, go ahead and procrastinate! With these tips, you can be productive while also indulging in your favorite procrastination activities. After all, why work hard when you can work smart?

37: HOW TO FORM TERRIBLE HABITS IN 21 DAYS

In this chapter, we'll explore how to form terrible habits in just 21 days. Who needs a healthy lifestyle when you can indulge in all your vices and live life on the edge? Forget about working out, eating nutritious foods, and getting enough sleep. That's for the weak and boring.

Step 1: Choose a Terrible Habit - Think about the habits you currently have and pick the worst one. Maybe it's eating junk food, smoking cigarettes, or procrastinating. Whatever it is, choose the habit that will have the most negative impact on your life.

Step 2: Do It Every Day - To form a terrible habit, you need to practice it every day. No exceptions. Even if you don't feel like it, force yourself to do it anyway. Eventually, it will become second nature.

Step 3: Don't Monitor Your Behavior - Whatever you do, don't monitor your behavior or track your progress. This way, you'll have no idea how much damage you're doing to yourself. The less self-aware you are, the easier it will be to continue your terrible habit.

By following these steps, you can form a terrible habit in just 21 days. So, go ahead and embrace what you know you really want to do - it's much more fun than forming good habits anyway!

ATOMIC BAD HABITS

CONCLUSION

Ladies and gentlemen, congratulations on reaching the end of this book. You have just completed yet another self-help book that promises to transform your life. And let me tell you, you've wasted your time. You've spent the last few hours reading about how to transform your life and become an average person, and let's be honest, you could have spent that time binge-watching your favorite TV show instead.

Let's be real, this book was just a bunch of fluff and nonsense, designed to make you feel good about yourself and distract you from the fact that your life is a complete mess. But don't worry, you're not alone. Billions of people's lives are a mess and somehow the world keeps turning.

Don't get me wrong, the author of this book is a genius. They have managed to somehow package common sense advice into a shiny new package, and you fell for it. But let's be real here, did you really need a book to tell you how to "be average" and "make bad habits"? You're probably already an expert at that.

But remember. If all else fails, just remember that laughter is the best medicine. So go ahead, put down this book, and tune into some comedy. Trust us, it's a lot cheaper than therapy.

ABOUT THE AUTHOR

Steven Kadlec is a self-appointed self-help guru, life coach, and productivity expert. He has spent countless hours studying the habits of unsuccessful people and compiling his findings into a book that he hopes will motivate millions of people into their most mediocre lives.

He attributes this to his "rebellious spirit" and refusal to conform to societal norms.

In his free time, Kadlec enjoys taking long walks on the beach and contemplating the meaning of life. He also has a crippling addiction to social media and spends more time scrolling through Instagram than he cares to admit.

Kadlec is a graduate of a prestigious university that he won't name-drop here because he doesn't want to come across as pretentious. He is also a certified life coach, which means he has paid a lot of money to attend a weekend seminar and receive a certificate that he proudly displays on his bedroom wall.

Despite his many flaws and lack of actual qualifications, Kadlec is confident that his book will change the world and inspire millions of people to become average.

Printed in Great Britain
by Amazon

ac6e3cd6-a398-4a75-b95e-949cac9dbba1R01